WEAVING
THE
WILDWOOD

Also by Alexandria Blaelock

FICTION
That Love Nonsense
Taipan vs Brown
The Ghost and Ms Cox
Friends Like That

SHORT STORY COLLECTIONS
The Haunting of Hayward Hall
Lovelorn, Lovestruck and Love at First Sight
Common or Garden Variety Heroes
Case Files of the Wilkinson National Detective Agency
Unavoidable Fates
Christmas Travesties
Five Faces of Felicia Clarke
Little Place Called Home
Security Directorate Dossiers v1

MS BLAELOCK'S BOOKS
Stress Free Dinner Parties
Signature Wardrobe Planning
Holistic Personal Finance
Minimally Viable Housekeeping
Planning a Life Worth Living

SELECTED SHORT STORIES
Alma's Grace
Bygone Boyfriend
Christmas Bonanza
Fate in Your Hands
Kiss of Death
Lady of the Looking Glass
Love in the Security Directorate
Morning Star, Evening Star, Superstar
Payton's Run
Secret Singer
Shining Star
Ship in a Bottle
The Shadow Thieves
The Palace Hotel
The Pseudonym's Bride

WEAVING THE WILDWOOD

A SHORT NOVEL

ALEXANDRIA BLAELOCK

BlueMere Books
MELBOURNE, AUSTRALIA

For permission requests, please contact enquiries@bluemerebooks.com.

Ordering Information:
Discounts are available on quantity purchases. For details, contact orders@bluemerebooks.com.

Weaving the Wildwood/Alexandria Blaelock
hardback ISBN: 978-1-922744-90-6
paperback ISBN: 978-1-922744-91-3
digital ISBN: 978-1-922744-92-0
AI generated audio: 978-1-922744-93-7

Book Layout © BookDesignTemplates.com
Cover Art © grandfailure/Depositphotos

For Nathan, who introduced me to the trees

into the forest I go to lose my mind and find my soul.

– JOHN MUIR

1

Alison Porter was on a mission to collect an emergency printing job.

Driving the tiny steel grey company car along tree lined secondary roads (because they don't have traffic lights), and a little over the speed limit (because it was an emergency).

Jamming the brakes on when she saw the red and yellow For Sale sign.

Stopping to look at the overgrown street frontage.

She wouldn't have noticed the property without the sign.

Even potentially with the sign.

Despite having spent the last few months looking for something she could afford to buy on her tiny salary.

Having developed the ability to spot a *For Sale* sign three hundred metres away at sixty-five kilometres per hour.

Or given her penchant for speeding, even more than five kilometres per hour over the speed limit.

And in any case, this sign was designed to be noticed

A quick watch check told her she had a little time to spare (the unexamined benefit of speeding), so she pulled over, parked on the verge, and power-walked up the steep drive.

The weather-beaten raw plank house was towards the back of the block. The placement was odd enough to make her think it was part of a larger parcel of land sold away in drips and drabs by past generations.

Unusually, the block hadn't been significantly cleared or cultivated.

Alison paused to imagine the delight of living within intact virgin forest as she surveyed the impenetrable vista of grey peeling trunks, pastelly minty green leaves, and the odd yellow nut that hadn't yet fallen away in the last season.

The tiny cottage sat on the smallest possible package of cleared land, protected, perhaps from the forest, by an old battered, twisted, and partly decayed three-bar post and rail fence, with a squared off arch over the gate that reminded her of a Japanese shrine.

Underneath it, a wooden sign naming the property "Crow Cottage" hung by one of a pair of chains, the other nowhere to be seen.

A path led under the arch and into the forest.

She knocked on the weirdly large and brightly coloured scarlet door, hoping to score a guided tour, but luck was not with her.

The short walk up the drive had reminded her it was a stiflingly hot day. A grove of eucalyptus trees cast their dappled shade over the sun-faded tin roof, and this, along with the cottage's retro details, was equally charming.

Not completely in love with the front door, which looked faintly ridiculous against the weather-greyed planks.

Did not even notice the pendant light hanging above the door, festooned with cobwebs as it was.

Taking a step back from the door, she looked along the wide, apparently sound wooden planks of the verandah fronting the house. After double checking to be sure no one was watching, she walked along it.

The exterior looked to date from the early twentieth century. As she circled the verandah, peering through the windows, it looked as though the interior dated from that time too. Had someone abandoned the house?

It was all too easy to imagine her friends trying to hide their jealousy as they sipped cocktails on the verandah, watching the sun set on warm summer evenings.

And somewhat more prosaically, as she realised she was looking at an old-fashioned pulley clothesline system. So she imagined hanging her washing under cover on rainy days too.

Alison guessed it would take a lot of time and money to update the property to modern standards, which would scare off buyers. And that would place it squarely within her inadequate price bracket.

She called the agent.

Who agreed to meet her on her way back from the printers to show her around.

A couple of hours later, she was inside, looking around. Surprised to find the house was cool inside, thanks to the high ceilings and low thermal properties of the unfinished floorboards. It didn't smell stale or mouldy, and all the walls and windows appeared intact.

The cottage wasn't exactly huge. At the front, there was a combined kitchen (with electric appliances), diner and lounge facing north to the street. At the back, two good size bedrooms and a large one room bathroom, including the toilet.

The pipes clanked and hissed, grudgingly producing both hot and cold water. Though it would probably require boiling as well as purifying before drinking.

The wood heater in the centre of the public rooms promised cosy winter evenings drinking hot chocolate as she snuggled under a blanket to read.

All set on ten acres of dense, lush bush land.

Sure, it was run down. The wallpaper reminded her of maps found in epic fantasy novels and would have to go (because it was giving her a headache), but that wasn't much of a deterrent.

Alison was young and energetic (or so she thought, though people younger than her would've snorted at her self-definition). It wouldn't take long to give the place a thorough clean and a lick of paint.

And even luckier for her, the property was close to a National Park. And that meant stringent planning and building controls that would deter property developers.

She finished her tour and put an offer in.

A cheeky bid, well below the asking price.

And was delighted, rather than suspicious, when the vendors accepted without negotiation.

She assumed it was a deceased estate, thanking her lucky stars for squabbling children desperate to sell.

Stretching her luck, she asked if she could move in early, and they said yes.

Without charging her any rent!

The agent set a date, and she happily gave notice on her rental.

Opened a new page in her already bulging bullet journal for a house to-do/buy list, and started packing.

First on the list, get rid of the wallpaper; she couldn't look at that every morning while she made coffee.

2

Taking advantage of her boss's attendance at a one-day workshop, and Hump Day ennui, Alison took Wednesday off and got the move done at the cheaper midweek rates.

Early that morning, she finished packing the last of the boxes to be collected, and slid them across the floor to wait for the removalist.

While she waited for the van to arrive, she packed a couple of boxes of "first things" into her little lemon yellow hatchback, and felt the butterflies multiplying in her stomach.

Stroking her hands down the sides of her favourite black-and-white striped t-shirt, hoping its feel good inspiration would get her through the day.

While at the same time, worrying she'd end up ruining it.

The removal van was all packed up within half an hour, so she raced it to her new home.

Arriving at the house, taking a pre-emptive moment to enjoy being a homeowner, before slotting her key into the lock. She turned the key, threw open the font door and found nothing had changed since the viewing.

Her brain stopped working for a moment.

(You might like to imagine an endless wait in a broken down elevator with the most annoying, tinny, on-hold music you can barely tolerate piped in to get an idea of what she was experiencing. Though she interpreted it as a minor episode of tinnitus).

The previous owners hadn't cleaned the cottage.

Or removed the furniture.

The stunningly hideous Victorian mahogany furniture.

With only one coffee in her belly before packing up the coffeemaker, all she could see were problems without solutions.

Without another coffee, she didn't think she could even begin to start thinking about how to deal with all the problems multiplying like rabbits.

So much for Ms Cool and Efficient Executive Assistant.

When it came to work, if you had a problem, Alison was your girl. Whether it was someone to call, or someone to do, Alison could take care of it all with barely a pause to slick back her hair.

But, confronted with a house full of someone else's furniture to move, her mind just went completely blank.

Panic rising, she shut the door and turned her back on it.

Then closed her eyes and took a deep breath, holding it for ten heartbeats (after her shoulders dropped, but before she passed out).

One thing at a time.

The owner's furniture bulked out the place in a way her tiny apartment's worth of flatpack specials could only dream of.

Plus, it would save her from buying anything substantial in the meantime.

Maybe they'd let her have it and she could on-sell it.

Or remove the most of the hideousness with a small crowbar or saw.

As she let her breath out in a whoosh, she turned around, reopened the door, and flicked the internal light switch next to it.

It flickered wildly for a moment, then blew.

Perhaps it *would* have been more sensible to get the electrics and gas checked *before* she moved in, but it was too late now.

Cursing, she scrabbled for her phone and lit the torch before opening the closest curtains. Enveloping herself in a cloud of dust so dense she had difficulty breathing as she struggled to find her way back to the front door.

As she emerged from the cloud, she didn't notice the cobwebbed light over the door was still alight, while the internal ones were not.

After a few deep breaths of clean air, she opened the rest of the curtains. And after running outside to take a few more, struggled to figure out how to open the double-hung windows to get some fresh air circulating as the choking dust settled.

She was sure it hadn't been that bad when she inspected, though the agent had opened the house before she got there...

The desire to vacuum waged war with the knowledge she'd left her cleaning supplies at the flat so she could clean it before turning in the keys - no sense to leaving money on the table when she'd need it later.

In the same line of reasoning, she rifled through her "first things" boxes to find the contract of sale. Which unhelpfully said nothing specific about contents left within the house.

And after a quick phone internet search to confirm, she confirmed as she'd moved in before the property settled, the furniture still belonged to the previous owners.

And rang the agent, leaving a message asking him to confirm a removal date with the owners.

Then found and opened the fuse box, to realise she had no idea what she was looking at. Except it seemed about the same age as the house, and would almost certainly need updating.

A small wire-wrapped card in the box's bottom gave her the idea the fix had something to do with the wire, but she didn't know what to do with that either.

She'd need an electrician.

And an electrician checking the services would most likely find some other issue that would need time (and money), and probably a complete rewire of the entire house.

Which admittedly was small, though the corresponding bill would most likely not be as small as she hoped.

As she'd moved in early, she now had some doubt over whether she or the owners were responsible for getting the electricity sorted out, and whether she'd be able to get the owners to do anything at all about it.

After all, they were selling, and probably just wanted the money.

She added light globes and surge protectors to her to-do/buy list.

With the removal truck backing up to the house, there was no more time for research.

She dumped the phone in her neat, compact, rectangular black leather handbag, and went out to welcome the removalist.

A young guy ran round the back of the truck and started opening it, while an older approached her.

"G'day love, where do you want it?"

"I've a bit of a problem," she said, hands on her hips. "The previous owners haven't taken their stuff out yet."

"Ah, is that so?" He thought for a bit, rubbing the stubble on his chin, "tell you what, let's take a look."

He walked through the house, assessing the situation. "It's old, but all good quality furniture, better than yours, if you don't mind me saying."

Alison smiled faintly. She'd figured that out on her own.

"Look, the bedrooms are a good size - they made them to fit dozens in those days. How about we move as much furniture as we can into one bedroom, then stack the rest up at the lounge end of the house? We can at least give you one bedroom more or less ready to go."

Until that point, it had seemed vital that Alison get all her things into the house, but somehow, with the removal guy making the extra effort, her furniture looked more like firewood chock full of toxic chemicals.

"Let's just move the bedroom furniture and leave it at that," she said.

He smiled, "good girl," and patted her shoulder.

She grimaced; she was not good, nor was she a girl.

But he was old enough to label all women girls, presumably in the firm belief it was a compliment, so she let it go.

Happily, the removalist was as good as his word, and soon enough she was paying the bill and waving them away as the boy backed out of the drive.

At least the place didn't seem overly crowded with her stuff there. Though she had the sense her smooth featureless flatpack furniture made the rest of the house and the furniture uncomfortable.

Fair enough, now that she could see it against "proper" furniture, it made her uncomfortable too.

Much as she'd have liked to pause to savour the moment of becoming a heavily mortgaged home owner, it was still early in the day, so she left the house, closing and locking the door behind her.

After stopping for a much needed take out latte, she returned to the apartment and gave it a quick clean before returning the keys.

It would've been much nicer if she didn't have to clean the new place as well when she got home.

But at least Alison had a quiet moment to relish being a homeowner.

A heavily mortgaged home owner, but a homeowner nonetheless.

And as a new homeowner, her enormous bath would still be there when she got home. And could luxuriate properly.

The "old" property taken care of, she stopped at her favourite noodle restaurant for one last box of noodles with whatever that fizzy foreign drink was.

As she sat at a table, waiting for her food, she fully appreciated the folly of carefully locking her new home's door but leaving the windows wide open.

Not something she'd worried about much in her third story walk-up apartment.

She added window locks to her to-do/buy list.

And while she was thinking about it, grabbed her phone and watched a bunch of "how to replace blown fuse wire" videos. Enough to leave her confident she could take care of that small repair herself.

By the time she got back to the house, the butterflies in her stomach had multiplied so many times she thought she might be sick.

On tenterhooks, she stood in the doorway, but nothing had changed. Not even the dust floating in the air.

Alison's shoulders dropped as she let out the breath she hadn't realised she was holding and relaxed.

Being a homeowner was nerve-wracking.

She brought all her cleaning gear into the house and started cleaning all over again.

First thing; the bathroom.

The taps ran with rust-coloured water for quite some time before finally running clear. The ancient hot water system groaned and wheezed as it eventually came on, but the tap did, eventually, produce an adequate amount of steaming hot water.

She added a hot water system to the do/buy list.

And trotted to the kitchen to put a pot on the stove to boil to see if it still worked. Fortunately, it did not blow up as she'd half expected it to.

Though it made the whole glossy red front door thing seem even more ridiculous.

Maybe they'd bought it secondhand and installed it just in time for the sale.

She got an extra hour or so of cleaning done, emptying bucket after bucket of filthy black water down the drain before she called it quits.

And by that time, all she wanted was a quick, hot shower.

Which was when she realised the bathroom did *not* have a shower.

Nor did it have any tap attachments for a washing machine. Not that she had one because her old apartment building had one for the tenants.

She sighed and wondered how much that would cost and whether it was too late to back out.

After two glasses of white wine, and an excellent pack of fish and chips from a local chippy (conveniently across the road from a coin-operated laundry), she went to bed and slept fitfully.

Crow Cottage creaked and settled as it cooled and contracted overnight. Noises that were startlingly different from the sounds of the brick apartment building Alison had left behind.

As was the noise of creatures scurrying outside in the forest. Or perhaps more properly, the wildwood.

The branches scraping the roof in the slight breeze, and the frightening pounding of possum feet as they ran across the roof, hissing and grunting.

Still, as things often do after a sleepless night, everything seemed a little more positive in the morning.

Because she was a homeowner!

Even allowing for the ghastly fantasy map wallpaper.

Which didn't seem quite as ghastly in the morning light.

In fact, it seemed quite charming; more like a medieval world map, albeit a world that didn't look like the one she knew. One with tiny houses and streets that seemed to get larger when she focused her attention on them.

For the first time, she asked herself why they'd wallpapered the main wall while the rest of the walls remained undressed. Given it was an interior wall, it couldn't be for insulation, could it?

Alison had been in the habit of putting some coffee on to brew in the morning while she took a shower. So while she appreciated the extra shower-free time for a leisurely breakfast on the verandah, not showering left her feeling sticky and wrong-footed.

But as she stood on the verandah at quarter to seven, looking out into the bright blue, cloudless summer sky, overall, she felt quite positive about choosing to buy the cottage.

And moving into it.

And on balance, she hadn't *really* missed her shower.

Nor was she particularly bothered by the necessity of minimalist make-up because the spotted bathroom mirror was so tiny she could barely see her face in it.

Or pulling her hair into a messy ponytail because there wasn't an electrical outlet in the bathroom to style it properly.

But maybe staying in a hotel while the cottage upgrades took place was a better option.

Not that she could afford a nice one.

Or indeed a not nice one.

Or anyone to do the bulk of the work...

It was also Alison's habit to catch public transport to work; it was cheaper, usually less stressful, and often quicker.

Besides, the aggravation of driving *before* she got to work had the tendency to last all day.

And on the odd occasion she missed the train, there were delays or cancellations, it reminded her boss and colleagues how much they needed her.

But best of all, it gave her a bit of quiet uninterrupted time to relax, read a book or listen to a podcast.

So, adjusting the fall of her black all-season wool pant suit, wriggling her toes in her hot pink suede ballet flats, and adjusting the placement of her boxy handbag over her shoulder, she prepared to leave for work.

As she stepped off the verandah, a big black crow dropped to the top of the shrine arch and tilted its head to inspect her closely.

She shuddered. "One for sorrow," she quoted her superstitious mother.

In spite of that, she squared her shoulders and walked under the Crow Cottage arch and out into the eucalypt forest between the house towards the street.

As Alison walked down the path, deeper into the trees, she enjoyed the sunlight slanting through the branches, feeling them towering above her. The slightest of breeze shook the trees enough to rain leaves down on her gently.

Like confetti. Or maybe blessings.

She stopped to fill her lungs with a deep breath of fresh morning scented eucalyptus. Didn't notice the path had petered out to nothing, and she was finding her own way through the trees.

As she walked on, she enjoyed the forest's beauty. Perhaps enjoying the knowledge it belonged to her even more.

It was available to her for as long as she owned the cottage. And on balance, that was looking to be about as long as she lived.

But as she descended the hill, she started thinking it was taking a hell of a long time to get to the street.

And she couldn't hear any traffic noise.

Nor did there seem to be any birds, crows or otherwise.

She turned to look back at the house, and it wasn't there.

Her feet stopped moving.

Of course, the house was there. It was probably just something to do with the angle of elevation, and she simply couldn't see it.

Not even the ridiculously red door, and given she was looking at grey trunks, seemed a little less ridiculous.

Alison turned and started walked further down hill again, before wondering if she was, in fact, walking down the hill at all. Couldn't she have maybe drifted to more of a perpendicular path?

As she stopped to look around for landmarks, she noticed pine trees in the middle of her eucalypt forest.

Not that she could recall seeing them as she looked out from the verandah. The eucalypts were tall, but were they tall enough to screen the pines?

Acknowledging her current situation might be considered "lost," she drew her mind back to more pertinent considerations.

If she had drifted to the perpendicular, and *if* she kept going, she'd probably walk into a fence and follow it down to the road.

Taking a second to think, she decided not to bother writing clear up the garden or install a path on her to-do/buy list, reasoning there was no chance she'd forget about getting lost in her own front yard.

As if to mock her, somewhere far off, a lone crow called.

Which made her feel better (about not being alone). Though at the same time she felt worse (it was an unattractive call, making her think of crows picking through corpses on the battlefield).

The pine trees surrounding her were uniformly dark grey in the weak morning sunshine, not a skerrick of moss on any side to guide her.

Not that she knew whether to walk towards or away from the moss, but she knew it was important.

Something about the sun.

But the sun had disappeared. The gaps between the trees were full of the foggy cloud you get when the winter sun hasn't fully cleared the horizon, so that was no help either.

And also decidedly odd, given she distinctly remembered standing on the verandah appreciating the view, featuring the bright blue sky you only get when the summer sun is high up in it.

And she hadn't noticed when it started clouding over.

Alison realised she was cold and needed to get out of the creepy wildwood and into the sunshine to warm up.

Humphing, she grabbed her phone and attempted to open her map app. At one bar, the signal was very weak, and almost as soon as she connected and got the app open, the battery died.

She sighed and put the phone back in her bag.

This was the kind of aggravation she could do without. The kind of aggravation she caught the train to avoid.

Fortunately, she kept a charger on her desk for exactly that kind of emergency. Even if her boss used it more than her. And he was the real reason it was there, though other people availed themselves of it. And she was generally fine with that, as long as they left their phones there and didn't take the charger away.

She sighed and scratched her neck.

Wouldn't the easiest option be to go back to following the slope of the hill down until it met the road?

Torn, she looked at the lie of the land and the trees surrounding her, then picked a new bearing, and walked straight into a scruffy young man.

Given he was wearing a long, knee-length pleated shirt, (that might have been white at some point), over brown leggings tied with some kind of string, and a brown jerkin she deduced he'd been involved in some kind of re-enactment.

Probably passed out drunk somewhere after too many beers and was now walking home with a massive hangover.

He was about her height (shortish), with a triangular face, blue eyes, dark bushy beard, and full head of dark badly cut hair.

"I'm so sorry," Alison said, "I didn't see you."

He backed away from her, glancing down at her legs, then up to her chest, across her face and back down to the ground as though he wasn't sure where to look.

As though he worried it might be safer not to look her in the face.

Alison glanced down at her body, not finding any reason he might have thought that, except perhaps she had something on her face.

She swiped both hands across her face and back over her hair; it all felt okay - no mud or bird droppings or other suspicious substances.

She resisted the temptation to take her mirror out of her bag and check it.

"Are you okay?" she asked.

He nodded, not moving his gaze from the ground.

"Then I'll let you get back to it."

She moved to take a step around him, and he dropped to his knees, a pack she hadn't noticed falling to the ground beside him. He bent over so his head almost touched the ground and reached out to grab the hem of her pants. "Min Lady..."

Alison, startled into stillness, waited without moving or speaking.

"Min Lady, have thee seen mine grandfather?"

He was taking the whole re-enactment a little too seriously, though that was no reason not to help him.

"Er, no," she said. "Would you like me to help you look?"

"Non min lady! Thee cannot concern thou-self with ain peasant."

Definitely taking the re-enactment too seriously.

"Well, um... Then, I'll be on my way."

And this time, he let her go.

Alison walked a few steps before her conscience got the better of her.

"Are you really sure?" she asked, turning around to discover the man had risen, got his gear together, and sloped off into the bush as though he had never been there at all.

Silently.

No scuffles, footsteps or crunching leaves. No sound whatsoever.

She looked to the right and the left, even scanning up into the trees and around at the ground, but found no trace of him.

Surely she ought to have heard *something* as he scarpered.

And then jumped, thinking he must be a pickpocket, and rifled through her bag.

Happily, it all seemed to be where she'd left it; no additions or subtractions.

Sighing, she looked around again, realising she was lost again.

Or still lost.

Childishly, she closed her eyes and spun around and around until she didn't know which direction she was pointing at before she took another step. After all, one direction was as good as any other.

Ridiculously lost in her own front garden.

She took another step, and then another, and one more before a horn blared and something fast and heavy roared past.

Startled by the sound of a car horn, she opened her eyes and found herself about to step onto the edge of the road.

Squeaking, she walked backwards a few steps off the road.

Wanting to sit down on the kerb.

Badly.

What the hell had just happened?

Out of habit, she went for her phone to check the time; impossibly, 6:45, the same day.

And then she remembered, equally impossibly, how her phone had run out of battery halfway down the hill.

The only reasonable explanation was that half-asleep, she'd sleep walked down the hill, dreaming an incredibly vivid dream.

It was in no way a reasonable explanation, but it was the only explanation she was willing to tolerate.

4

During the course of another hectic day, Alison background obsessed about her experience in the garden that morning.

Allowing herself to believe she'd dreamt it.

Or let her imagination get way too carried away by the romance of her new home.

And after all, ten acres of bush *is* a lot of land to get lost in.

But that evening, standing at the foot of the property as dusk settled in, she wasn't so sure.

There was no sign of any kind of path through the wilderness, even though she knew it was there at the other end, along with an arch and a sign.

At war with herself, she looked backwards and forwards between the long, straight driveway and the seemingly virgin bush.

Tempted to chicken out and use the drive.

But Alison was stubborn.

Bloody-mindedly stubborn.

It was that bloody-minded stubbornness that had taken her from an underqualified administration assistant in a small plumbing business to a well-paid Executive Assistant working for the Chief Executive of a medium-sized firm, supervising a small administration team.

She'd managed the purchase and fit-out of their new office. Then the consolidation of three satellite offices into the new one. And the installation and upgrade of new software.

She was pretty sure she could bloody well find her way through her own front garden.

But, by five steps in, it had all started going horribly wrong.

And by the time she chickened out and decided to walk up the drive, it was too late. She was stranded in the featureless wildwood once more.

No sign of the drive.

No sign of the road.

And no sign of the stupid, but as it turned out, the incredibly necessary red front door.

Reasoning it worked that morning, she closed her eyes, spun around, and took five steps before opening her eyes again to see nothing familiar.

False bravado, she thought to herself.

Or maybe sunk cost fallacy.

Not that she had any real choice but to continue, snorting at the idea of calling in a helicopter rescue team to find her.

In her own front yard.

She'd never live that down.

Or manage to pay for it.

But just in case, she checked the charge on her phone, finding it dead once again.

Figured.

She probably hadn't properly plugged it into the charger.

Stupid, stupid, stupid.

Swallowing, straightening her spine, she fixed her focus on a tree directly uphill of her and hiked up to it.

Then picked another tree and hiked up to that.

Until she came across an empty open wagon.

It was made of large wooden planks resting on a thick, square axle connecting the two sets of two metal rimmed spoked wooden wheels.

The woodwork was old and weathered, scratched and dented. The tray was covered with a carpet of leaves, giving Alison the impression it had been there a while. Though she couldn't tell whether there was anything wrong with it or why they'd abandoned it.

A dried rutted track led to (or from) the wheels, but there were no tracks or droppings to suggest the horses or oxen that drew it had recently been uncoupled and led away.

Given the size and weight of the wagon, she figured you'd need a team of eight or ten powerful men to replace the non-human animals that drew it.

Did it have anything to do with the man she'd met that morning? Or had someone else dumped it? That morning, or a decade ago?

Or maybe it was just a rather large and unexpected garden feature.

The track led uphill, which was in the direction she wanted to go. And it wasn't like she had a map, or compass, or anything useful for finding her way. So, it wasn't hard to choose to indulge her curiosity and follow the tracks back to the source, hoping it would lead past her front door.

Because it'd been an hour since she'd left work and she was keen to get home to use the bathroom. And since she'd got lost (again) in her own front garden (again), pour herself a bucket full of wine.

Hoisting her bag more firmly up her shoulders (telling herself she needed to stop carrying so much junk) she ploughed on, expecting to find the end of the track relatively quickly.

Or, given the morning's encounter, meet someone along the way.

But as the seconds ticked by, in the silence, save for her feet swishing through the leaves, she was feeling the slightest bit dispirited.

Not a breath of wind stirring the leaves, no creatures on the ground or in the sky.

As if the world was holding its breath.

Alison, the woman who boldly walked, half-drunk, along the inner city streets in the middle of the night on her own, stopped feeling dispirited and started feeling uneasy.

Ducking glances behind her and across to either side, listening intently for indications anyone was following her.

Not really concerned about animals; as far as she knew, the only thing she had to worry about was an enraged kangaroo or perhaps a feral pig, cat, or dog.

She stopped, glancing around her, thinking she'd heard something rustling in the bushes.

But it fell silent, so she started walking again, persuading herself it was an echo of her movement from the trees.

Stopping suddenly, just to make sure.

Still nothing.

She closed her eyes and took a deep breath; her imagination was getting out of control.

This was her land. She had every right to be there, and nothing was going to scare her away.

She let her breath out and started walking before she opened her eyes.

When she opened them, she saw her fence, along with the stupid lopsided sign and the stupid red front door.

Two crows sat on the arch.

She smiled grimly; two for joy.

Certainly an apt description for Alison's feelings at that exact moment as she scrambled the rest of the way, reaching for her key as she did.

Once she arrived at the verandah, she looked around; half-sure she was being paranoid, half-convinced someone was following her, and an extra half convinced there was something different about the house.

As if she could actually tell after just one night of living in it.

There wasn't anything obvious about the look, so maybe it was just the strange red light of dusk.

But she was sure there was something different about the smell; something smoky and woodsy. Or perhaps it was a man's deep, earthy cologne.

She eased the key into the red door, listening through it, almost certain she could hear someone moving about inside the house.

Instantly thinking of the re-enactment guy.

Half afraid, and half outraged, she threw the door open so hard it ricochetted off the wall and slammed shut in her face.

But for a moment, she could've sworn the view from the door was a large, open hall with a fire blazing in the middle. There was just enough time to note a white bearded man with a bunch of people wearing furs standing around the fire talking.

Alison blinked, and looked at the door, less inclined to open it and more inclined to ask for her deposit back before discretely retreating.

Feeling overly imaginative and utterly ridiculous, she looked up and rubbed her eyes to force the burgeoning tears back into them. Shifted her footing, grounding herself more securely on the verandah, and steeled herself to open the door once more.

She opened the door a crack and peered inside.

The monstrous Victorian furniture was exactly where she'd left it. Which ought to have reassured her, yet it did not.

5

After visiting the bathroom, Alison got changed and poured herself an enormous glass of white wine. Drank half of it, then threw a tea towel over her shoulder and started chopping lettuce, tomato, capsicum, cucumber and red onion for a Greek salad.

As far as she knew, moving into a house wasn't supposed to be this difficult.

At least three other women in her office had somehow managed moving recently, all of them managing not to get lost in their front gardens.

Though none of them were living on more than pocket-sized five hundred square metre blocks. Neither did they have anything more than a mini strip of lawn between the street and the house.

What she really needed was a map.

Wondering, she turned and looked at the wallpaper. Was it a map of the garden?

Wiping her hands on the towel, she backed up to the front door to take in the expanse of the wallpaper map.

There wasn't an obvious repeat in the pattern, which was encouraging.

Given the cottage was at the rear of the block, she searched the top edge first, but sadly found nothing labelled Crow Cottage.

Or anything that resembled a compass to tell her which direction was North.

So, if not on the edges, the next logical place would've been in the centre, but she didn't see it there either.

Then again, it was an enormous map.

Did it represent more than the ten acres she'd bought?

A lot of the original land grants were split into smaller parcels, distributed to the heirs, or sold off for housing subdivisions.

And there were a lot of huge modern houses on little blocks surrounding the property she now owned.

She opened up the map app on her phone, (miraculously fully charged and with a good strong signal), searched for her place, and compared the phone to the wall.

There didn't seem to be much similarity between the two. She swallowed a glug of wine, zoomed in and out, rotating her phone as she looked at the wall, trying to find something to orient herself.

She was about to give up when she found something on the bottom left of the wall, next to the door of the bedroom she was using.

It was so teensy; she had to get down on her hands and knees before sliding down to her belly. Resting her chin on her folded hands, to think about it.

According to the wallpaper (if you could believe it), the cottage was an unnamed outlying farmlet. The scale, such as it was, suggested just the house, not the ten acres.

Annoyingly, it appeared the rest of the property was off the map, somewhere beneath the floorboards.

Then again, the house seemed to point towards the rest of the map, so maybe not.

No matter how she looked at it, the crucial question about whether the map would be useful for negotiating the wildwood in the front garden remained unclear.

Continuing to stare, she wondered who left the wagon and why?

Was it supposed to keep her out, or stop something worse from coming in? What, if anything, would be worse?

Alison rolled on her back to look up at the ceiling and think about how she could explore the garden.

Aside from chopping all the trees down.

One thing was sure, with all those crows, crumbs *à la* Hansel and Gretel would not do the trick.

A ball of string like Theseus?

Though any concrete marker she left would be available for others (like the medieval re-enactors) to use. Or destroy, while she was away, so strings might not be the best idea.

Wayfinding was, of course, possible, though stars weren't best known for being visible during the day.

The last option was to mark the actual trees. Painting or carving the trunks. Maybe hammering plastic markers into them or poles into their bases. Tying the branches with tape, or piling up rocks between them.

She seemed to recall someone had invented some kind of system for marking trees, or more properly, blazing a trail, so she'd have to look into that.

Could she get some spray paint?

Something else to add to her to-do/buy list.

Was it likely the re-enactors had already blazed the trees? Would they follow any blazes she made?

More importantly, could she make enough sense of the wallpaper map to take it inside the wildwood and put the correct marks in the right places?

6

The next day, Friday, would be a busy day, in which Alison'd need her wits about her to minute the board meeting.

Not one in which she wanted to battle the garden.

Driving to work seemed the lesser of two evils.

Keeping her eyes firmly on the ground, she ran under the crow gate to the car, backing up and turning the car without looking at it.

Not that it helped, it turned out to be a tough day, regardless.

As the meeting broke for lunch, her boss led the chattering board members out of the meeting room.

The catered lunch was, as usual, waiting on a trolley outside the room. Alison made a grab for it to push it into the room and lay it out on the table.

Her boss detached himself, and said, "by the way, I've run out of ink," waggling his pen at her, "could you get me another?"

She nodded. "Sure, I'll just bring the catering in."

"It's fine, I'll do it," he replied, and took hold of the trolley.

Her boss preferred a particular brand of disposable roll-erball pen, so she maintained a secret stash, because he was always losing them.

But her secret stash was empty and there were none in the main stationery cupboard.

As she ransacked the office looking for a pen, she suddenly realised she hadn't investigated the contents of the furniture left in the house.

Perhaps there was a more useful map in one of the pieces of furniture.

Or something like a painted landscape picture or photo, to help make sense of the garden.

It wasn't her furniture, so the idea of opening it and going through the contents made her skin crawl.

The last time she'd opened a drawer that didn't belong to her, she'd found something children should never have to see; an experience that made her highly resistant to doing it again.

But the owners had left all that old mahogany furniture unattended in the cottage, so they couldn't complain if she rummaged through it.

Could they?

If she was careful, and if she put everything back where it came from, they might never know.

The more she thought about it, the more she realised there was a lot of furniture that might provide valuable clues.

She was about ready to dash off to investigate when her boss popped his head round the door, "I'm okay - I found another pen in my jacket."

After he'd left, she rolled her eyes at the wall. Thank heavens he was so disorganised - she'd almost abandoned the board meeting.

Needless to say, the rest of the meeting was torture, and she could not get home fast enough.

Nor could she help but see the three crows on the gate.

Three times a letter.

Was that a positive? As a child, she'd always thought so – what could be more exciting than a letter left in the mailbox for you to discover?

Alison unlocked the door, pausing to *see* all the old furniture.

How was it possible she'd forgotten how much furniture there actually was?

Thanks to the removalists, it was like a secondhand store; all jumbled up higgledy-piggledy at the far end of the lounge.

A buffet, desk, dressers, wardrobes, glass fronted bookshelves.

Having given herself permission to go through someone else's belongings, it was tempting to just dive straight in.

She made herself get changed first.

Brushed the dust off her "good" suit and hung it on a handy wall hook to air out. Gave her shoes a quick polish before putting them away.

Rang for a pizza, with a six-pack of beer on the side.

Watched the start of the TV news while she waited for the delivery, and the rest of the news as she ate.

Enjoying the suspense of wondering what she might find.

Only after she'd eaten and put her rubbish in the bin did she permit herself to start with the brass knob handled buffet. Where she found a lovely old set of china, some tarnished silver cutlery, and yellowed table linens.

Plus a tiny miniature oil portrait of an old man who looked vaguely familiar. A twinkle in his eye, and the suggestion of a smile made her feel she'd have liked him a great deal.

The drawers and wardrobe contained clothes (no surprise) though they didn't seem to conform to any one time frame.

An early twentieth century suit hung side-by-side with a quilted doublet and hose. Cheek by jowl with an elaborately embroidered coat, vest and lace shirt.

There was even a silvery jumpsuit that put her in mind of a space suit, or Ziggy Stardust costume.

All approximately man sized, for a man who perhaps attended a lot of costume parties.

And going by the quality of the costumes, a fairly wealthy man at that.

Wrinkling her nose, she surmised the old man in the portrait was a Hellfire Club member, dressing up for a night of debauchery.

The bookshelves were full of antique books, written in Latin on thick parchment pages. Alison couldn't read them, but she hauled a couple of massive books out of the case and onto the desk so she could flip through the pages.

Nothing hidden between the pages, no diagrams as such, just two columns of densely written handwriting or type.

If nothing else, when the time came, if the owners didn't claim them, she could sell them.

Which left the desk, eight sets of locking drawers stacked one on another in columns on both sides, with one thinner, wider drawer above the space for the knees.

While the desk was still ornamented, by comparison with the buffet, it was plainly finished.

She tried the drawers, one at a time, first the left and then the right, all of them still locked.

Happily, the last one, over the knees, opened, and she started pulling the contents out; bottles of dried up ink, a couple of bone-handled fountain pens with a dozen or so spare nibs. A letter opener with a matching magnifying glass and paper cutter. A couple of used sticks of sealing wax, along with a seal featuring the outline of a bird.

It wasn't too far of a stretch to imagine it was a crow.

And most importantly, a brass key, which she immediately tried in the top drawer on the right to reveal a selection of papers and envelopes.

Then systematically opened all the others; a scale with niches for the balancing weights in the base. Alison was surprised all the weights were still there.

Thick brown wrapping paper, previously used and folded up for reuse along with a couple of half used balls of string.

A candle holder and a couple of sticks, an ashtray with a match holder.

And a collection of letters bound in string.

Alison paused, debating morals again, before pulling the string off and shuffling through the envelopes.

All addressed to M, at Crow Cottage, which seemed both mysterious and suspicious at the same time.

When she opened the first letter, signed Q, Alison was annoyed to find it in code. As was the second, a random letter from further back in the pile, and the one on the bottom.

It was going to take more patience than she had at the time, and more brain power than she had to spare to break the code, so she set the letters aside for another day.

7

The next day, so far as she could, Alison followed her usual Saturday routine; shopping, laundry, cleaning.

Though that day, she put her clothes on to wash at a laundromat while she visited the market. And when she got home, hung her new hammock on the porch, climbed into it and ate a couple of rice paper rolls from the market.

It was going to be a wonderful place to relax.

However, there was no time for relaxing, so she gave the cottage a quick tidy, and prepared to explore the garden.

Packing a backpack with her phone, some water, a first aid kit, a penknife, a compact red down jacket, a couple of muesli bars and some chocolate.

Throwing in a little cash, just in case she ended up somewhere that wouldn't take a phone mediated electronic transfer.

Dressed in her old blue jeans and a faded long sleeved denim shirt, shoving her feet into sturdy hiking boots and tying the laces tight.

She felt slightly ridiculous taking luggage with her to visit her own garden, but as she'd got lost several times, it seemed a sensible precaution to take water and snacks with her.

She had the idea of mapping her route, so took a new notebook and a pen, nothing the departure time (as she walked under the gate and started along the path) as half-past twelve.

Four crows on the arch; four something better.

Though what would be better?

So far, so good.

One path, one direction, more or less straight ahead.

Planning to look back at the cottage every few paces to work out where she lost sight of it.

Approximately ten steps in, she looked back along the path to find the house and gate were gone.

Not out of sight due to changes in elevation, but out of sight with no sign they had ever been there.

Instead, the path behind her stretched out, gently curving to her right.

And further up the hill, seemingly in the wrong direction, was the wagon she'd seen on Thursday evening. Or one very like it.

Alison turned the notebook around, drew a line across the page, noting the length of ten paces. Then drew a backward arrow and marked the wagon.

She looked around at the ground and the trees, but saw nothing that suggested a blaze left by someone else.

Given the route to the house was seemingly unavailable by virtue of having disappeared (no need to panic just yet, she assured herself), it didn't seem worth marking it.

Trying not to worry about the house, she walked up to the wagon, reasoning that doing so would end up taking her to the street. After all, she'd found the wagon on her way back from the street.

She walked around it, not seeing anything different about it. The ground was scuffed up, as though someone had bogged it, and the ground had dried before anyone came to retrieve it.

Was it the same wagon?

The path curved to her right, and broadened, so she marked the directional change on her map and followed along.

A little later, she arrived at a cluster of four extensively fire damaged ruins on a crossroad.

Alison looked for distinguishing features. Marked the first quadrant of her map with a caved in roof, the second with a still standing porch, the third with a staircase, and the last with the two standing walls.

The ruin with the caved in roof didn't seem to have enough rubble for it to be more than one story. The scorching extended through to the garden with blackened remains of tree trunks, twisted fragments of metal, and mounds of ashes.

Thankfully, no obvious skeletons, human or otherwise.

The ruin wasn't warm to the touch or smoking, and the air was fresh and untainted by smoke. It was clear the house hadn't burned down within the last couple of days.

The other buildings were in more or less the same state.

Was it a wild fire? Or something worse?

Had the people left voluntarily after the disaster, or had they been driven out?

With the wildwood behind her, burnt out farmland in front of her, and nothing much visible from either side of the crossroad, it didn't matter which direction she followed. She tossed a coin; heads crosswise, tails ahead.

Heads.

She tossed the coin again; heads left and tails right.

Heads again.

But turning in that direction, she felt something unsettling, and found herself reluctant to continue in that direction. Just couldn't get over a feeling of doom and possible disaster.

She'd learned to trust her guts, so she walked back to the middle of the crossroad and closed her eyes. Shifting her feet backwards and forwards, facing first one direction, then the other.

There wasn't much to choose between them, and while the path to the right still felt like calamity, it felt like less of one.

So Alison marked the map, turned the notebook to match her direction, and walked to the right.

A gust of wind blew up behind her, and she paused to put on her jacket, taking a drink of water, unwrapping a muesli bar and shoving it in her mouth as she did.

Munching it as she continued on her way.

Feeling a sharp sting, she slapped her neck and dislodged a tiny, blue feathered dart.

Stumbling as whatever poison was in it entered her bloodstream.

Falling as it took effect.

8

It was dark when Alison woke.

She panicked. How was she going to find her way home now?

With great effort, she calmed her breathing, and forced herself into problem-solving mode.

She was lying on her side on a hard, but not rigid surface with her arms tied behind her, and her ankles tied together.

Stiff, but not in a great deal of pain.

Nothing much to hear, nothing much to see, no smells of cooking, mustiness or animals.

Was she inside or out?

Was it night-time, or was she blindfolded?

First point, not dead, and that alone was cheering. As she'd passed out, the thought of dying had been right there at the top of her mind.

So, good job not dying!

She wiggled her fingers and toes, just a little, so as not to alert anyone to her consciousness. It seemed all her extremities were still there, and still functional, so another win.

Second, so far as she could tell (without looking) she was still wearing her own clothes. Jeans, jacket, boots.

Presumably the red coat was as much a liability for her as it was for the English, when firearms became standard military issue - highly visible and easily killed at longer distances.

Still useful for rescue, though.

And back to the first point. Why was she still alive?

She leaned back, surprised to find her backpack still attached to her back.

Was that good news as well?

It seemed to still have its lumpy contents, so probably.

Okay then, not dead, not harmed, still in her clothes.

She leaned her head back and cleared her throat.

The sound didn't echo, and there were no noises to suggest anyone had heard or was moving towards her.

She tried moving her head along the ground to work out whether she had an incredibly well tied blindfold in place.

Indeterminate.

As was whether she was wearing earplugs or noise cancelling headphones.

Her mouth felt fine (as opposed to gagged), so why block her eyes and ears, but not her mouth?

The one thing she knew for sure; her map was useless right now as she had no idea where she was in relation to where she'd fallen.

Also, fairly sure, she was not in her garden any more.

When she'd looked at the wallpaper map, her house had been in the bottom left corner, and that left the rest of the wall.

Which was a lot considering how far she thought she'd walked.

Squeezing her blindfolded eyes shut to focus better, she tried to remember what else was near the bottom corner.

Had there been a crossroads?

Or farmland?

Or whatever the hell place she was now located in?

Just about the time she thought she'd go mad, something nudged her back.

She stiffened.

Something about her head relaxed. There was bright light, the sound of chaos, the smell of wood smoke and some kind of hearty soup with an undertone of unwashed bodies. Possibly animals as well.

It was enough to make her want to clap her hands over her ears, but she couldn't move them.

"Be still," a man said, "ipple wear off in ain moment."

Ah, the re-enactors were responsible.

Alison turned her head toward the voice, trying to focus despite the consoling tone.

His face swam into focus.

A strangely familiar blue eyed, bearded triangular face, under badly cut dark hair.

"You... You... You..."

Alison struggled to find something suitably loathsome to call him but came up empty.

"Yes min lady," he replied, "Ich."

Annoying as hell. But comforting to see a familiar face. Several other people surrounding her shuffled backwards out of her line of sight. Thinking if she couldn't see them, she couldn't curse them.

As her view sharpened, she could see she was in a structure made of raw wood planks. A couple of dark wooden chairs pushed up against one wall. In one of them sat a white bearded man in a blue tunic with a fur over his shoulders.

Thrones?

"Why have you brought me here?" she demanded.

The man she recognised answered, "we-self seek thy assisten benefit defeat the Rochand."

Alison attempted to get herself to her feet, but he laid a gentle hand on her shoulder, "Ich pray thee, stay down for thy benefit."

She paused, attempting to work out what he'd said, and he removed his hand. She deduced benefit meant safety.

"Surely ain witch as powerful as thee can assisten us win."

"Assist you how?"

"Enchauntment."

She looked around at the other people, "Ich'm non other enchaunting."

Dear god he was wearing off on her.

"But thee were lost in th' air!"

Somewhat harder to explain that she didn't know how she came to disappear. Also uncertain how to explain he was the one who disappeared, or whether that would work, either.

"I can't help you, I didn't do it on purpose—"

Whatever it was on her head tightened, and she could no longer see or hear anything.

9

Instantly Alison panicked, struggling to loosen her arms or separate her legs, but there was no give in the bindings.

Attempting to at least get to her knees, she was rewarded with a blow to her back that sent her face first to the floor again.

She cried out, and lay still, hoping she hadn't broken her nose, and not wanting another face plant.

Wagering with herself, she was back to the path on the left of her map, where the feeling of doom had overcome her.

Because, if she was on the less doomed right side, there was something even worse on its way.

Was it the Rochand?

And was the Rochand an animal, monster or human?

Regardless, what non-magical aid could she offer an assemblage who hoped to defeat whatever a Rochand was.

No connections as such to be made, but if they could give her the contacts, she could probably negotiate supplies of whatever it was they needed to defeat the Rochand.

Or visit markets and negotiate bulk purchases on their behalf.

If they were medieval re-enactors determined to stick with their roles as peasants, that would probably be food, uniforms and weapons.

Perhaps she could use fairs to mask the movement of said uniforms and weapons. Did they have the skills to pass as performers? Could they nick stuff while no one was look-ing like the gypsies were reputed to do?

Mind you, the Medieval period spanned a thousand years, between the black death in the fifth century and Christopher Columbus in the fifteenth, so maybe that wasn't all they needed.

Would they need hard currency in the form of pennies or were they still relying on barter?

But whatever it was that kept her senses masked seemed like pretty good magic, so why did they need her?

Wait, pretty good "magic"?

Yes, pretty good magic - she could not, for the life of her, come up with any kind of non-magical way to just cut her sensory input.

By which she meant technology because she did not be-lieve in magic, just science that she didn't understand. Which, it had to be said, was most of it.

Unless they'd slipped a balaclava over her head, and she would definitely have noticed that when it came off.

It was possible there was some rogue, not historically accurate stealth technology in use.

Then again, was there even such a thing as a stealth bal-aclava in her own time?

And if there was technology, would she be able to use it? Was there a universally compatible software stealth balaclava?

So aside from the technologist, were they all peasants? Or did they have some knights or other nobility in their forces? Priests, monks or friars. Not to mention nuns.

If they *were* actually medieval peasants, surely they'd believe God had put them in their place. They'd expect to live in misery, earning their reward in heaven.

Wouldn't they?

Unless it was post-Black Death, when they'd be negotiating pay increases (so to speak) or walking off the job.

So, *if* they were medieval peasants, it was more likely the Rochand was a monster than a man or animal.

And when exactly did she start thinking this was, in fact, some kind of medieval enclave situated in her front yard?

So back up a moment, there was still a possibility they (or some kind of disease) would kill her, so she had to come up with something she knew how to do and they didn't.

Aside from telling them to wash their bodies *and* the clothes they inherited from dead people to kill fleas and lice to keep them safe from the plague.

They probably already knew about defensive placements like mounds and ditches, with spears or pikes set in the bottom, and barricades on the mounds.

So, she probably *couldn't* offer them anything much that was useful.

Assuming they wouldn't let her go home to buy artillery weapons on the black market. And assuming she could, in fact, get them back to wherever the hell she was.

And whose brilliant idea was it to explore the front garden, anyway?

Or, let's just say for a moment, she had landed in Medieval England. Could the Rochand something to do with the Norman Conquest? The Count of Anjou outside his turf?

Vikings? Christian missionaries, Spanish inquisitors, Muslim invaders or a guerilla Pagan resistance?

Slavers, pirates, or Mongol hoards making a bid to cross the channel?

Some kind of disease mechanism (invisible without microscope, fleas or mosquitoes)?

Did they expect it to come by sea, horseback or foot?

Through fleas or human breath?

It was unfortunate she wasn't a minister who could perform a miracle to make the village disappear like Brigadoon.

Though if they were looking for a disappearing act, perhaps she could help them move. They'd need to backtrack to get the wagon for that, plus another one or two, as well as animals to draw them.

It might even be possible to get the villagers to Crow Cottage, then make it seem as though their village had never been there in the first place.

And once they got to Crow Cottage, maybe they could find a home in her place and time, or even use the grounds to move to another time.

Because once you got over being able to move from one place to another, it didn't seem likely that whatever technology had brought her to wherever she was, could only go in one direction to one place.

Would dressing it up as a pilgrimage make it more palatable for them?

Could they move further back in time rather than forward? Then they'd have time to prepare for the coming of the Rochand.

Aware she was winding herself up with the possibilities, she told herself, back up a bit and take a deep breath.

One thing at a time.

She was imprisoned, or at the very least, deprived of her freedom.

She did not know where she was, aside from having got there via her own front garden.

Should she suddenly have her freedom restored, she didn't know where to run or how to get home

So theoretically...

Theoretically...

Nope, no idea what theoretically.

Theoretically try to escape and get back home?

But she thought about the passably attractive man she'd met in the garden the other day.

It seemed he and his people were in need.

She still had no idea how to help them, but felt compelled to help them. Even if she wasn't a witch and couldn't disappear into thin air.

Though she could still read, but only modern English. Certainly not older Englishes, Latin, any of the Frenches or Germans. But perhaps reading phonetically aloud would be enough for someone else to decipher the text.

But as a reader, and a reader of Arabic numerals too, she could do a bit of maths too. Surely that would be helpful - arithmetic, trigonometry, financials and statistics?

No problem.

But probably not calculus, at least not without the help of the calculator on her phone.

Gift of God or not, she could read clocks too, and coordinate a logistics schedule of people and places to time, so that might be useful.

Aside from the whole not having an agreed calendar until the sixteenth century.

Or potatoes from the Incas, so no potato batteries.

Or chimneys, so maybe she could introduce them early.

Her basic first aid skills, using alcohol as an antiseptic, splinting and bandaging wounds, would be useful in the early medieval, and heresy in the later.

In any case, she hoped she wasn't still around in the time it would take to impress them.

And then again, they'd probably expect herbal poultices and teas if they thought she was a witch.

And that was more or less okay, as long as she didn't find herself burned at the stake for it.

And she didn't have to sniff chamber pots or worry about the four humours.

She could sew, kind of. And cook, as long as she didn't have to slaughter anything.

Plus five self-defence lessons worth of personal combat skills.

Was being an outsider a skill?

The techno-balaclava was taken off again.

10

The white bearded man stepped in front of Alison.

"Alfred here," he said, jerking his thumb behind him at the man she'd met previously, "thinks you can assist us, so we are going to take a chance on you."

Alison was so ecstatic to not be facing imminent death that the man's informal modern English didn't at first register.

"He offers his life as surety for yours, so if you run away, he will die. Do you understand?"

She nodded.

"Then set her free."

Someone behind her took a step forward and cut her bonds with one slash.

Alfred stepped forward and stooped, offering his hand to help her up. She smiled gratefully, staggering as the blood rushed to her hands and feet, but managed to stay standing.

Given the recognisable words in the command, she realised the elder's previous words had been too. And before she could debate the wisdom of it, blurted out, "uh, Sir have we met before?"

"I don't believe so," he took a step back, turning his face away.

"At Crow Cottage perhaps?"

He looked at her, brow furrowed for a long second.

"Leave us," he commanded, and aside from Alfred, the people disappeared.

The old man jerked his head, "you too, hop it."

When they were alone, he asked, "Who are you, and how do you know about Crow Cottage?"

"My name is Alison Porter, and I just moved in."

The colour drained from his face. "You just moved in? What year is it?"

"2022."

"2022?" He frowned, and spoke half to himself. "I've been gone a long time then."

Alison shifted her weight to her other foot. "Um, when were you last there?"

He noticed her discomfort. "Come, come," he said, gesturing to the chairs, "sit with me."

Then poured something from a jug resting on a table beside him into two bowls.

Alison sat and took the bowl he offered.

"Your good health," he toasted.

"Cheers," she raised the bowl towards him and took a cautious sip of something that tasted like a sweet desert wine; perhaps mead or something like blackberry wine.

Very much sweeter than she preferred.

"Now then," he said, "where to start?

"My name is Michael Trotter. I took the first two hundred acre grant of land in 1872. The allocation turned out to be good growing land, and I planted pine saplings close together, hoping to grow some tall, straight trees suitable for ship's masts."

Alison nodded, made sense. She took another sip of wine.

"After several years, the trees were growing well. One day, I went out to look at the trees to work out how much longer it would be before I could start the harvest. And I found myself," he waved an arm around him, "here."

"Here?" Alison asked, knowing she had to stop repeating what he said and ask a serious question, "where's here?"

"Ah, now there is another question, because the path through the pine plantation does not always end in the same place."

Michael took a sip of wine and continued, "the first time, I arrived in a fantastical tropical place of glass towers, the next a cold dense wilderness with enormous monsters. I had no option but to conclude that perhaps the forest is some kind of time portal."

Alison sagged in her chair. It was one thing to reason it, and quite another to have it confirmed. "Do you think it's always the same place? Are we in England?"

"Do you know I never stopped to consider that? I most certainly did not arrive anywhere I recognised, though I have also never arrived in a situation that did not speak English."

"And how do you control where you end up?"

He rubbed his face with a shaky hand. "As I am still here, I clearly do not know how to control it."

Then drained his bowl.

He was stuck then.

"Can you get back to the cottage?"

Michael sighed, "not anymore. I theorised that eating or drinking in this place loosens your connection to ours."

Alison nearly choked on her wine as she gasped, dropped the bowl, and started coughing.

She'd come this far, and now she was trapped here?

In what might as well be the faerie kingdom?

Michael pounded her back helpfully.

"I built the original house," he said wistfully, "and Queenie called it Crow Cottage as there always seemed to be crows about."

"Queenie?"

"My little Vixen. I loved her dearly, but her social standing was such that I could not marry her."

"You can't have loved her that much then," Alison said, head full of old romance novels.

He smiled with one side of his mouth, "perhaps in your time. I once visited a place where marriage was not permitted at all. People negotiated contracts for the provision of children, and somehow, the children were conceived and raised elsewhere."

Alison nodded, sounded far-fetched, but it wasn't that far removed from the surrogacy arrangements she was familiar with.

Which made her wonder, "were the saplings transported from England?"

"Yes."

Alison thought for a while. "I read an article where some scientists thought they'd proven some kind of communication link between plants in a forest; something about hormones or stuff in the roots. Is it possible the saplings have maintained a connection to the one they came from? In England?"

"I can see why you might think that. But how does it know when to send you?"

She signed, "I don't know, but if you're accepting trees can transport you to the other side of the planet, it's not much of a step further to have them send you in time."

"But how?"

"I blundered here twice, so let's think about that for a moment. The first time, I was trying to get to work, and I met Alfred and oh... Is he your grandson?"

"Yes, how did you know that?"

"When I saw him that day, he asked if I'd seen his grandfather. I wonder if it was him that summoned me..."

"I see. Then what happened?"

Alison continued, "oh yeah. Right. The second time I found a wagon when I was trying to get home, so I wonder if the wildwood brought me to a place it thought would help."

He grinned, "As a young man fresh off the boat from England, I landed in Australia looking for adventure, and I certainly found that in the forest."

"Right," Alison said, "then moving through time in the forest is probably the best way to escape the Rochand. I'd say an earlier time might be better than something more recent."

"Rochand?" Michael asked. "Oh of course, the Rochand. I had forgotten about him."

She looked at him quizzically, but he was looking up at the ceiling.

"I wonder could we fetch Queenie to come with us?"

This was not a question she'd expected. "No harm in trying. Assuming I haven't drunk enough faerie wine to keep me here."

"Faerie wine? Ah yes. Faerie wine indeed."

"Then let's go see what we can do."

He nodded and stood up. He leant towards her and she heard a sharp crack before he leant back, bundling something shimmery into a concealed pocket.

The stealth balaclava, no doubt.

"What is it?" she asked.

"Breathing apparatus from a long time in the future, though I suppose not that much longer for you."

"To go with the silver suit?"

"Ye— How would you know that?"

"I rifled through your wardrobe looking for clues."

"Why you..." he folded his arm back as if to strike her, and she balanced her feet in a defensive crouch.

"Impertinent girl."

She shrugged, "what's wrong old man? So far as I can tell, you abandoned the place."

His shoulders slumped. "I suppose it would look like that."

"Look," she said, attempting to placate him, "let's just see if we can get there, and then work out the logistics."

He nodded and led the way.

"Oh, and I think we should bring Alfred too."

He frowned at her, then shrugged.

"Wilfric," he bellowed, and a man stepped forward.

"We are taking a trip, and I do not know how long we will be. Please obtain wagons and pack everything in the village up. Be prepared to depart at a moment's notice."

Wilfric nodded and turned on his heel.

"Alfred," he shouted. His grandson popped up from somewhere, startling them both, "come with us," and strode off towards the forest.

Alison scurried to catch up.

11

After a quick march through the forest, Michael called a halt. "So far as I can tell," he said, "we are about where the border between the worlds begins."

Alison had seen nothing familiar about the walk, nor did she see anything familiar in the vicinity.

She wondered how up to date his knowledge of the wildwood was, but it couldn't possibly be any worse than hers. Taking him at his word, she looked closely about her; was that tree a little familiar?

She walked a little further, and the men followed her, a few steps behind.

But, the only thing she knew for certain, was that when she was lost in the wildwood, she'd closed her eyes and hoped desperately for sight of the cottage.

So she closed her eyes, thinking about the cottage and Michael's hope to find Queenie, took a step, and noticed a lightening in the forest's atmosphere.

She opened her eyes, and there it was.

With five crows on the gate; five for silver!

"Who hoo! We did it!" She said, turning to look behind her, finding she was alone.

She closed her eyes, pictured Michael, glowing with pride beside a shack he'd built. Still with her eyes closed, she reached out and someone took her hand. She pulled, and opening her eyes, found Michael standing before her.

Turning to look at the cottage again, aside from a woman sitting on the verandah in a long dress and dainty straw boater, cradling her face in her hands, the only difference was the door.

Made of individual planks held together with a cross brace, like a gate.

Michael saw the woman and shouted, "Queenie." She looked up as he ran to the verandah and embraced the startled woman.

She struggled for a moment, until he said, "oh Queenie, my love, how I have missed you."

Alison turned away to give them a moment to reconcile.

As she did, another crow settled on the gatepost.

Six for gold.

More than one kind of gold, she thought. What was *her* version of gold she wondered for a moment.

Pulling her backpack from her shoulders, she drank some water and ate some chocolate, before turning her thoughts to village sized things.

Could Michael bring the villagers through, or did it have to be her?

Would they have to do it one by one, or could they do it in conga line style (either with or without the dance)?.

Or, if they asked the wildwood nicely, could it move the entire village?

While the village was a modest collection of houses, would it damage the wood to collect and remove it?

Which led her to wonder whether anyone else had the same connection to the wildwood she seemed to share with Michael. Albert, for example.

At a guess, he'd been born into it, so ought to have a stronger connection to it.

Though he hadn't made it through to the cottage...

She stood up, thought about him, and reached out a hand. He grabbed it in both of his, and she pulled him through.

"Ich tolde thee thee coulde get lost in th' air," he said smiling.

And that answered that question. Sort of.

He nodded at her, then looked around him, and walked off to examine the enclosed clearing more closely.

Maybe he just needed to learn how to navigate the wildwood.

Come to think of it, would a compass help her navigate it? Though if the wildwood wasn't attached to a given time, was it attached to a given place? Was there a root of some kind that bound it some place in the universe?

Something to consider if she ever got out of whenever she was now, but in the meantime, she needed to get the lovebirds organised.

"I know we've seemingly got all the time in the world to plan the village disappearing act, but we've got to get organised."

12

R ather than taking care of the planning himself, Michael seemed happy to let Alison and Alfred take care of it.

Instead, he took Queenie inside the cottage, and when Alfred went to follow, Alison laid a hand on his arm and shook her head.

"I'm guessing your grandfather is hoping for a little privacy right now."

He tilted his head, "Ich do non-other understand."

She smiled, "to be alone. Except for Queenie."

He shook his head, but remained outside the cottage.

She sat on the edge of the verandah and patted a spot beside her. "How many people are in your village?"

"Five families, so about fifty folks."

"And how many animals?"

"Mmm, oxen, bleet, pigs, cattle, and poultry. Ich don't know, maybe tens ophe ten."

So what, a hundred?

"And how many wagons of grain and household items?"

He shrugged, clearly struggling to quantify the relevant details.

Not to worry, she didn't know what the wildwood could do.

As she sat looking out at it, she got the idea she should ask it.

"Wait here," she told Alfred, and walked under the arch and ten steps into the forest.

She looked back to make sure she couldn't see the cottage, and then sat, making herself comfortable against a pine tree, conveniently stripped of its lower branches.

She wasn't exactly sure how to convey what she wanted to know, or how she'd know when she'd received her answer, but that did not deter her.

Taking deep breaths, and slowing her mind, she imagined the village as she remembered it, and the forest encircling the village. Keeping it safe as the Rochand, imagined as a hoard of tree burning nut jobs, attacked the village.

The wildwood shuddered, in the way she thought a coop full of chickens might shudder at an approaching fox.

She thought a reply came as a vision of herself leading a caravan of people, wagons and assorted beasts from the village into the wildwood.

From which she deduced the wildwood couldn't save the village unless the villagers sought refuge within it.

Odd as it felt to trust the wildwood had responded to her message with one of its own, it wasn't actually any odder than anything else that had happened that day.

Was it only a day?

Surely it had been longer than that?

No point checking her phone, and she hadn't brought a watch, so no point looking for that either.

All she had to do now was get back to the cottage, collect Michael and Alfred, and return to the village.

Alison crawled out from under the tree, her limbs so stiff she thought she might've sat there for a hundred years. And looking at the vegetation growth she had to fight her way through, she was sure of it.

She stood up and staggered towards the cottage. Strangely, she knew exactly *when* she had to go to find the others.

13

Somehow managing not to fall over, Alison lurched under the gate. "All right people," she croaked, then cleared her throat and tried again, "All right people, let's get ready to go."

Alfred burst out of the cottage, "where-as-ever have thee been? Thee have been away for weeks!"

Michael and Queenie weren't far behind, also demanding to know where she'd been.

"I was in the wildwood," she said, "asking the trees how we could move the village."

"You look done in poor love," said Queenie. "Surely you have time for a cup of tea, at least before you go?"

Alison wondered if a cup of tea would be enough to trap her in that time. Without consciously thinking about it, she reached her mind out into the wildwood, feeling rather than hearing the whisper of leaves.

Which suggested time to rest and drink tea was not a bad thing.

And as she dearly needed a strong cup of tea, she nodded, and half collapsed. Sliding down a verandah post to the floor, leaning her weight against the pole to wait as Queenie bustled into the cottage.

Weeks, Alfred had said, she'd been gone for weeks!

She closed her eyes to rest them.

And bolted awake three days later, to the urgent sound of rustling leaves. "Hurry," they seemed to say, "you're almost out of time."

"Time to go!" she shouted, "we've waited too long."

Michael and Alfred were ready, but no sign of Queenie.

"Queenie's not coming?"

Michael sniffed. "Queenie is too fond of modern luxuries," he said, and Alison wondered what luxuries exactly Queenie had in mind that she was unwilling to leave.

"I'm sorry," Alison said. And she was, even though Alfred was evidence Michael had found someone else in the meantime.

"At least I know now," he replied.

"I can try to check in on her later if you like."

He shrugged. "She's made her choice, and I won't have to wonder what it would've been anymore."

"Okay then. Is there anything you want from the cottage?"

He waved a small carpet bag. "If it was good enough for Phileas Fogg, then it's good enough for me."

She raised an eyebrow, "gold sovereigns," he said.

Should she have been more concerned about the time line?

Maybe, but there was a village that needed loading into wagons before she led them pied piper style into the wildwood.

Besides, by the time anyone came to do an archaeological dig in or around the village, the metal parts of the bag would've corroded, perhaps leaving the archaeologist to make up a charming story about the gift of some kind of pin.

And as for the sovereigns, if not melted or worn down, chances are they'd be interpreted for exactly what they were. A stash of gold sovereigns buried in the ground for safekeeping.

"Then we're ready to go?"

The men nodded in the affirmative.

She closed her eyes as she passed under the arch. Concentrating on enclosing the men in a bubble of imagination as she felt her way through the wildwood. Aiming for a time she hoped would be before the Rochand overcame the village.

14

The trip seemed to take a long time. Alison could feel the men's restlessness and doubt, thinking perhaps they were walking with their eyes open. Willing them not to say anything in case they broke her tenuous connection with the wildood.

She couldn't help imagining what the fallout might be if they arrived too late. And on that scary thought, she felt a kind of bump, staggered to a stop and opened her eyes.

The village was within her line of sight, and as she caught the smell of smoke, the men ran on ahead of her.

The village itself was fine, but the smoke was a taste of what was to come. Alison looked along the road, but couldn't see any sign of warriors aside from the smoke.

The main question was who was burning the fields; people fleeing from other villagers or the invaders. That the smoke didn't contain the taint of meat was reassuring.

The wildwood reached out to her, its alarm increasing her agitation.

Wilfric was shouting instructions, and Michael and Alfred lent their voices, encouraging people to hurry. It seemed to take forever to finalise the start of a column.

Alfred appeared, "we-self art ready for th' first wagon benefit move ahead."

Alison nodded. "Once I move, I'm not sure I can stop without losing the path."

He nodded, "Ich understand," he said, squeezing her shoulder.

And louder, for the benefit of the villagers, "follow th' witch!"

Which on the one hand was true, but given what she knew about witch finders, wasn't much comfort.

Then again, witch finders didn't arrive until the seventeenth century, presumably as a way to put down uppity women and reclaim the patriarchy's losses after centuries of plague and upset.

What would Michael and Alfred have made of that?

The column behind her started walking, and she opened herself to let the spirit of the wildwood guide her once more.

Her eyes were open, but she didn't see the wood in front of her. She saw strings of golden light in and around the tree trunks, binding them together.

She looked down at herself and saw golden strings connecting her to the wildwood. As she watched, they shot back towards the caravan of villagers, through the villagers and onto the oxen pulling the wagons piled with grains, the pigs, sheep, cattle and chickens.

Satisfied she had them all, she started walking, and the column followed behind.

It felt like very slow going, though the tree's feedback felt almost faster than she could bear, and she wondered would she be able to keep it together to guide them safely through the wildwood.

The caravan proceeded in almost complete silence. The people glanced over their shoulders and whispered quietly as they walked, holding the hands with lovers and children lest they get lost.

Even the animals held their peace, as if they too knew how important it was to get away undetected.

And then the last wagon got bogged in the dung and piss of the preceding wagons.

"Hold up," someone called, "wagon bogged."

Alison didn't know where they were in the wildwood, or even if they were safe, but if the wagon was bogged, it had to unloaded, and either reloaded on the remaining wagons, or carried by the villagers.

She stopped, fighting as the golden strings dimmed to keep the connection with a wood that was afraid of the invaders.

Wavering as Michael grabbed her shoulders, gently shaking her. "Hold on there my girl. We will not take long. You are a *good* girl. You *can* do it You *can* make it."

A small, tucked away part of her laughed to be encouraged like a disobedient puppy in training.

But she felt a little stronger, and as if the wildwood was encouraged as well, the golden strings brightened.

She had no idea how Michael's quiet voice had kept her in thrall, or what they had done with the contents of the bogged wagon, but eventually he let her shoulders go, "you can walk on now."

And she did.

Following the golden strings until they ran out.

And she fell, exhausted and insensible, to the ground.

15

The caravan had arrived at an abandoned village, with exactly the right amount of houses and yards. Whether it was their village, or was it some other village, no one could tell for sure.

They had lost nothing on the way; not one person, not one chicken, not even a single grain of cereal.

The villagers rejoiced, settling in and preparing a grand feast to celebrate. They lit a bonfire using a pile of dead trees, blown down in some storm near the new village, slaughtered a sheep and roasted it over the fire with vegetables and beer to wash it down.

Meanwhile, Alison did not wake up.

Over the next few days, the villagers took it in turns to pray and watch over her. Bathing her feverish body with cool, clear water.

Until a week later, the fever broke, and she woke up.

The villagers were ecstatic, but all she wanted to do was go home.

Michael tried to dissuade her, but she said "Faerie food," and he let her go.

The village assembled to bid her farewell, but she was agitated and wanted to be on her way, terrified she wouldn't be able to leave at all.

She smiled, and hugged and thanked all for their good wishes, but she knew the wildwood was impatient to be done with her as she left the village alone.

"You have done a good thing, Alison," Michael said. "You have saved my village, and you have saved me from a lifetime of regret, too. I hope you live a long and happy life in Crown Cottage, and I hope we see you again, too."

She stumbled into the trees, blinded by her tears.

But almost as eager to leave the village and be out of the wildwood as she felt the wildwood was to be done with her.

She couldn't see the golden strings anymore, but didn't need to see them or to close her eyes. She just followed a path that opened up and led almost immediately to Crow Cottage.

As she arrived, and understood where she was, she turned back to the wildwood, and bowed deeply. Trying to put all her thanks and gratitude into a burst of energy she hoped would feed it.

Adding in a little regret and nostalgia, along with her fervent hope the wildwood would stay in touch.

And turned back to the cottage.

16

Alison staggered under the arch, falling to the ground, utterly exhausted.

Seven crows watched her from its top.

Seven for a secret, never to be told.

She lay on the ground, rejoicing in the absence of movement as the noonday sun shone warm against her back.

As the spirit of the wildwood left her, it seemed her bones melted and she sank further into the ground.

Missing the sense of being something larger and more necessary than herself alone.

But she knew the wildwood remained just outside the gate.

Waiting for her next visit.

Perhaps Alfred was waiting too.

After a few minutes, the sun had lent her enough energy to crawl herself to her feet and slog her way to the ridiculously red front door.

The beautiful, comforting, welcoming red door.

Grateful and thankful for its existance.

More grateful to see it than anything else.

Except maybe her new hammock, which she was inclined to climb into and take a nap.

Or should she take a long, hot bath to wash the stress of her adventure away?

Not that it mattered.

She had the rest of her life to enjoy Crow Cottage.

And the forest.

And a secret never to be told.

THE END

ABOUT THE AUTHOR

Alexandria Blaelock writes stories, some of them for *Ellery Queen's Mystery Magazine* and *Pulphouse Fiction Magazine*.

She's also written five self-help books applying business techniques to personal matters like getting dressed, cleaning house, and feeding your friends.

Discover more at www.alexandriablaelock.com.